Emmanuels' Prayer

PAUL H. SUTHERLAND

UTOPIA PRESS · TRAVERSE CITY, MICHIGAN

UTOPIA
PRESS

111 Cass Street
Traverse City, MI 49684
pub@utopiapress.com
www.utopiapress.com

Library of Congress Cataloguing-in-Publication Data

Sutherland, Paul H.
Emmanuel's prayer/by Paul H. Sutherland.
—Traverse City, MI: Utopia Press, 2006.

p. ; cm.

ISBN-13: 978-0-9661060-6-0
ISBN: 0-9661060-6-7
Originally published as *Agnostic Prayer*
(Karuna Press, 2004).

1. Spirituality—Fiction. 2. Faith—Fiction.
3. God—Proof—Fiction. 4. Metaphysics—Fiction.
I. Title. II. Agnostic prayer.

PS3619.U844 E46 2006
813.6—dc22   0601

"One Love" poem on page 50 reprinted by permission.

Cover painting, *Assisi and the Patchwork Plains,*
© Debra Clemente, www.artistdeb.com

Book illustrations by Paul H. Sutherland
Book design by Aimé Merizon

For Those Who Pray
and
For Those Who Act

How can I be
so bold about love?
How can I with
confidence and optimism
say such truths about love?

Simple really...

I met my true love.

Quiet

I WAS BORN a desperately shy man. I had an insatiable appetite for knowledge; I wanted to know everything. Thus, well suited for a life of studying books and professorial lectures, I attended university. I rarely talked to people even when spoken to. If I was at a café guzzling coffee and eating my daily 100 gram dark chocolate Lindt bar, I'd ignore anyone who tried to engage me in conversation. My sage was prose.

For money I made sketches and sold them to a pompous gallery owner. He indulged a fantasy that he was as talented as the great Chinese GongBi painters who drew intricate drawings filled with extravagant color. He paid me well and never let me into his backroom studio. I thought he was an idiot and took my money and left. I had sufficient cash for tuition, rooms in simple hotels, coffee, and chocolate.

Between semesters, I checked into a new hotel using a specific routine. Approaching the front desk, I stared at the receptionist, held up seven fingers and circled them around my head. Then, I laid out seven stacks of money, each representing a night's stay, and stood there looking into the receptionist's eyes. She or he attempted to talk to me, sometimes bringing in the manager, but I just stared. Soon they handed me a registration form on which I drew seven suns and seven moons. On the signature line I wrote as big as would fit: Emmanuel.

Key in hand, I was escorted to my room where I unplugged the phones, TV, and radio. On the hotel's complimentary stationery I scribbled, "flowers, please," and handed it to the bellman along with the room's phone, TV, and radio. The usual result was daisies, irises, mums, or roses vased properly and placed quietly each day in my room.

Within 3,471 days, I earned PhDs in medicine, philosophy, physics, economics, fine arts, and English. Once I completed the course work and a 343-page thesis, I would drop it off at the professor's office with a harsh critique of each instructor and the school. I signed each final portfolio "Cynically Desperate," and never waited for any diplomas.

After six non-PhDs, I quit the world of fantasy, theory, and study.

Belief

PROFESSORS' WORDS and bookish distractions had given a safe, comfortable rythm to my life that I had not been aware of. Without the security of my university schedule I struggled to fill the emptiness. I had created a life that required goal-setting for motivation. I wrote in journals and sketched dark scenes about my fraudulent life that sought knowledge, facts, and theories. My years of university cloistering was little more than waiting for the sun to set in the east.

In complete despair I set out to prove that God did (or did not) exist. Each day I went to a church, synagogue, temple or spiritual edifice and sat outside sketching. Often, a "holy" person belonging to that religious tomb would seek me out. They quietly approached, usually curious about my art or eager to evangelize. Before they could speak, I asked, "What must I believe to belong to your church?"

Well-rehearsed sounds of salvation, redemption, sin, and heaven would spill from their lips into my ears. Once I was convinced they had spilled their religion raw, I asked my host, "Do you believe in gravity?"

I got another explanation that gravity is real and not a belief, like faith in God. I stared the pastor or priest or nun in the eyes and counted silently to 50. I then asked, "If God is real, why do I need to *believe* in God? Doesn't God exist regardless of my beliefs?"

I remained silent and continued drawing. The religious person would usually move on. After weeks of this, I became despondent from hearing only simplistic answers to my query, "What must I believe?" All their words were as meaningless as those spoken by my 74 PhD instructors, 84 college lecturers, and 17 primary teachers.

According to my numbered sketches, paintings, and journals, I visited 348 different churches in 172 different towns, chatting with 275 different "patrons of belief" from 38 different Christian, Islamic and Jewish sects. I also consumed 780 Cokes, 1,438 lattes and 367 dark chocolate Lindt bars without any greater understanding of faith or God's existence. The only effect was physical as blood appeared in my toilet water with great regularity.

Desperation

I FELT 50% LESS than human because I could not
get "faith." Perhaps faith was something you pretended to believe in until deluded into *believing faith
was real.* The emptiness and despair within me was
so overwhelming that I quit drawing. I made a pact
with myself to determine once and for all: "Is there
a God?"

I went to sell my final sketches to the pompous
idiot gallery owner in Venice. Finding his front door
locked, I entered through his studio where I discov-
ered my drawings re-painted. The clean lines of my
charcoal and ink sketches were colored in, modeling
a garish imitation of the GongBi masters. My face
burned. Anger raced through my veins. For a moment I savored this primal hate experience, but then
my bowels released a splurge of brown and blood as
chronic stomach pains convulsed me to the floor.
I coughed a deep red and remember falling into my

own vivid green, brown, and red pool.

I woke up in the hospital with IVs in my arms and a raging fire in my abdomen. I curled in a primal position. Ulcers, colitis, appendicitis, or diverticulitis—I had a stomach eroded by stress, chocolate, coffee, and Coke. After cycles of morphine and electrolites with raw stitches along my navel, I discharged myself, fueled by an anger so strong I found comfort in its power.

Death

BY THE TIME I was on the street in front of the
hospital I knew I must confront the idiot Wannabe
GongBi, the re-creator of my art. I stormed about
looking for a geographic marker and realized I was
in a most unfamiliar place. All the signs were in
French and I remembered my attendants spoke it
too. Heavily drugged for pain, I hallucinated that
I was left for dead on a vegetable truck bound for
France. My sutures were raw and I noticed I was in
a hospital robe; my sketches were hospital charts.
Through fading consciousness I read, "Name:
Unknown. Religion: Undeclared."

I woke up to "Good morning, Sir," from a nurse
who was chatting with another woman holding a
cell phone to her ear. While the nurse ran to get
the doctor, the Cell Phone Mama continued her
conversation. I scanned my situation: IVs in each

arm, left IV was saline and the right antibiotics, pain relief drip attached to the saline, my body and arms were held down with Velcro. Noticing the pain drip control, I squeezed it mightily, and, as my consciousness faded, I overheard the nurse tell the doctor, "I think he is Italian and a monk because he talks at night about colors, sketches, Venice, and God, so maybe he is Christian, too."

Each night an old woman with pure white hair entered my hospital room and softly prayed while holding my strapped-down hand. I kept my eyes closed and pretended to be unconscious. I was so weary that I couldn't bear the idea of regaining consciousness or looking into anyone's face, so I listened to the old lady's prayers, feeling comfort from her wrinkly cool hands enveloping my own.

One day around 10 a.m., the Cell Phone Mama wandered into my room babbling on the phone about "this boy who was found sick in my mother's garden," and how "he wants to die but I won't let him," and "fate, pity, compassion, do the right thing, and listen to your mother, I love you, blah, blah, blah."

My spell in the hospital further resolved me to

the pact I made regarding "Is there a God?" Until I could conclusively answer the question I would act deaf and dumb and do nothing on my own behalf. The hospital was not going to be helpful to my cause with IVs, food tubes, catheters, and attentive nurses. I thought, *I could be here forever.*

Late one night I opened my eyes and shook my body. When the nurse came in I looked at my Velcro straps and she removed them. I held my hand up to my mouth and she gave me water. She left the room to get a doctor and I grabbed my chart. I had been in the hospital six months, "Name: Unknown" with a note, "Confidentially, bills to be sent to 1011 Rue de St. Paul." I put the chart back before the nurse returned, doctor in tow. He proceeded to ask me question after question while I lay there, for all appearances mute and deaf. Finally, he said to the nurse in French, "His fate is his; your pity is not helpful!" She shrugged and they walked away discussing head injuries, luck, and ulcers.

I dressed and walked out of the hospital as if invisible. I went directly to 1011 Rue de St. Paul to find an abandoned cottage with only a musty bed. Lying down, I thought, *If God exists, I will not die.*

I awoke before sunup the next morning to find the night-visiting Old Woman staring me in the face. She gave me a coffee and a chocolate bar and left. She returned the next morning to find the coffee and chocolate untouched. I picked them up and consumed them in her presence. She said nothing, left more coffee and chocolate, and disappeared into the backyard. Always she would pray over me, holding my hand in hers while placing her other hand on my heart.

One morning she came to me with paper, pens, colored pencils, and an easel. She showed me an article about a man in Italy who had killed an artist "by accident" outside the gallery he owned in Venice, confessing that he hid the limp body on a vegetable truck bound for Paris.

The woman put the easel on my lap, carefully laid with thick white paper and gave me a pen. She said, "I wish for you to write down this prayer." She repeated the same prayer to me as she had for many nights now. I sat silent, pretending not to understand. Handing me coffee and chocolate, she left.

For the next 87 days she would repeat the easel, prayer, coffee, and chocolate routine until one day, as I stared blankly at her, she picked up a broom and beat me, starting with my legs and ending with my head. I passed out to her screams of "Destiny! Responsibility! Expression!"

Expression

I WOKE UP in the same hospital bed I had occupied months before. Sitting by me was the Cell Phone Mama, who held my hand and said, "What were you doing in my mother's house?" She explained that she was the caretaker of her mother's home as she pulled out an artist's portfolio containing a dozen pictures, sketched in my style, all showing the Old Woman who appeared at night with coffee and chocolate. She asked if she could keep them.

I shrugged, "Why not?"

Desperate to leave the hospital, I asked if she would get me clothing and shoes. "Were you the man from Venice left for dead?" she asked.

I wondered outloud, "Am I dead?" Cell Phone Mama left as I pondered my situation.

I didn't feel dead. I felt 150% alive. I could feel my heart beat. I felt completely empty and translucent. Colors were intense, the air moist, I wondered if I had gone mad.

Cell Phone Mama returned, bringing fresh clothes and shoes, and a backpack filled with art supplies, paper, and a compact easel. She thanked me for the pictures and asked that I come to visit her. I fondled the colored pencils and ran my hand across the warm paper, feeling its grain. I smiled, "I need to get to Venice." She smiled back that she understood.

I felt compelled to claim my PhDs and one by one, each school's proctor, whom I had slandered, gave me my certificate and said, "I knew you would be back."

Next, I went to the idiot's old studio to discover it was empty and for lease. I phoned the landlord and met him straight away. He agreed to let me live in the small apartment above the gallery space and allow me to show my work in the gallery below in exchange for one quarter of my art sales.

Feeling hungry, I walked to a central square to draw and sell a few sketches for my dinner. Money in hand, I bought bananas, coffee, and chocolate to last me a week and went back to my studio to sketch and paint.

In the gallery I never put price tags on my paintings and would accept offers only if I liked the person who made them. When wealthy American collectors came to town, I demanded $10,000 in U.S. dollars for my paintings. $20,000 to $40,000 came in each week.

I wrote on the back of each painting: "I read the sages: Jesus, Plato, Moses, and others too. I have found nothing superior to silence. Study is not the way; doing is. Do not mistake chatter for action. Pity helps no one. Compassion fills no stomach. —Dedicated to the Old Woman," or "—Dedicated to my beating," or "—Dedicated to Cell Phone Mama" and then I signed each one: "Dr. Emmanuel."

Six framed PhDs checkered my studio wall. I was completely immersed in my work; painting, drawing, sketching 12 to 14 hours daily. I took two hours each day to visit a café and eat chocolate, coffee, blueberries, and a plain spinach salad with tomatoes and cheese. As I ate I watched children play in a nearby park. I burned my books and only read my watch. I limited myself to 12 spoken words a day.

Soft Kiss

ONE DAY A YOUNG WOMAN walked up to me during my café meal, introduced herself as Mary Elizabeth Onle, handed me an envelope and kissed me ever so softly on the cheek saying, "I found this in my Grandma's stuff." Written in French on the envelope was:

Dearest Ellie, when you find this envelope, please take it to Venice and go to the Swedenborg café where you will see a handsome man around 40, eating chocolate and coffee. The chocolate will be a Lindt dark chocolate bar. Kiss him softly as you give him this letter.

The letter felt thick and I marveled at Mary Elizabeth Onle's duty-bound behavior. The rest of the note said:

Ellie, get on your knees and tell Emmanuel you will not leave unless he promises to write the enclosed poem on the back of each of his paintings and sketches. Don't move until he consents, even if he stays there forever. He is a kind man, but a fool who knows God and hides his light under his fear. He rarely speaks but I know he will speak to you.

I opened the letter now, curious about its contents. As I started to read the prayer another envelope fell to the ground. I continued reading:

Direct my actions, my consciousness and the very essence of my being to bring peace, harmony, love, joy, prosperity, health, and happiness to...

I looked up at Mary Elizabeth and said, "This is the Old Woman's prayer, it's some kind of trick. What happened to the old lady who beat me?"

The young woman was crying. I reached out to hug her and stumbled to my knees on the concrete patio. She tried to speak, but tears choked her throat. I felt a strange pain in my heart as I held her. Finally she looked into my face and whispered, "Grandma's been dead for ten years."

I shoved the envelopes in my pocket and, holding Mary Elizabeth Onle's hand, walked silently to my studio.

In my apartment we talked late into the night until Mary Elizabeth started yawning. I tucked her into bed, where she slept curled up like a small child. The envelopes were still in my pocket and I read the prayer again:

Direct my actions, my consciousness and the very essence of my being to bring peace, harmony, love, joy, prosperity, health and happiness to all sentient beings in the North, South, East, and West, above and below, both seen and unseen.

Dear Emmanuel, there were in my life many deep spiritual friends—right-action agnostics; love-conquers-all Christians; law-abiding faithful Jews; mystical practicing Muslims; and happy do-noharm Buddhists. This prayer changed our lives in such a meaningful way that we were able to take the basket off our light. Please speak. Please share your life with others. Please share this prayer.

The other envelope had a note that said:

Emmanuel, take Ellie to the spot on the enclosed map and bring along 64 colored pencils, pens, paper, wine, cheese, and a blanket.

Mary Elizabeth Onle stirred awake and I showed her my letter. As she showered and dressed, I went off to buy wine and cheese to throw into my backpack with a blanket for our journey.

I came home to find Mary Elizabeth dressed in my pants tied tightly around her waist, my cotton sweater was pulled over her light frame. She was napping on my only chair, a monster of a chair, ugly and black but very comfortable. I had never watched a woman sleep and found myself transfixed by her soft breaths that moved her breasts against my sweater and tugged gently at the drawstring on her claimed pants.

I pulled out my pen and sketched four poses before she was startled upright by the evening bells of the neighboring church. She smiled at me with eyes that seemed to see straight into my soul and said, "Please call me Ellie."

"CALL ME ELLIE."

Ellie

THE NEXT MORNING she laughed when I suggested we take a taxi the 50 kilometers we estimated our trip would take. "Do you drive?" she asked.

I said, "No."

She laughed so hard that she lost her breath. I had never laughed like that.

"Six PhDs and you can't drive!" She ran ahead of me, "Let's rent a car and I'll drive. Do you have money?"

"Yes, plenty," I explained.

"Then this is our car," she said, pointing to a red convertible Mercedes. With the top down, Ellie drove wildly towards our destination with loud American music blaring and a brilliant Italian sun on our faces.

Ellie stopped at each church we passed and went inside to pray. I wanted to know what she prayed and when asked she said, "You know, my Grandma used to tell me that we don't *believe* in God, we *know* God."

She looked up at the sky and called, "Thank you for Emmanuel who reminded me that God is." Then she glanced at me and said, "I don't know what I'll pray at the next church." With that she took the car to 150 kph and screamed over the wind, "Isn't this a grand adventure?"

Ellie slowed down a bit and asked why I had chosen to be a monk or minister or priest or whatever. "What?!" I yelled.

She said, "Aren't you a monk or something? You never talk, act like you're deaf and rarely look at people."

"I'm not a monk," I said, "I'm just a stupid man on a wild ride with a beautiful girl."

She slammed on the brakes and turned sharply into another church parking lot. She smiled, grabbed my hand and said, "Come pray with me!"

I said, "I have never been in a church before."

"Impossible," she said, "I saw your drawings, I counted 223 different church paintings and sketches, all with notes on them, like, 'God is, so I am.'"

I stuttered, "But, I never..."

"I liked your prayer drawings," she interrupted, "tell me about them."

"I'm afraid you might laugh. Can I wait in the car while you go pray?" I pleaded.

A bright streak crept up Ellie's neck until her whole face was red. She gave me a stony look and stormed into the church. Three hours later she came out, got behind the wheel and blurted, "You're a pompous ass!" She tried to drive but couldn't because tears blurred her eyes. She blundered out of the car and ran back into the church. I followed her. My heart raced as I got closer to the wooden, brass-lined doors.

I stopped at the doorstep, paralyzed and sweating, but I couldn't retreat so I just stood there. A moment later the door cracked and one of Ellie's wet eyes stared at me. She reached her hand through and pulled me in. We went to the front of the nave, she knelt, and I followed. Holding my hand tight, Ellie said, "I do not understand, dear God. Is Emmanuel afraid to show his light or is he selfish?" The afternoon sun streamed through colored glass and danced on Ellie's hair. For the first time in my life, I was crying.

Minutes Become Hours Become Days

ELLIE AND I KNELT there for at least an hour. She prayed. I cried and sweated and my mind emptied into my body and my body seemed to flow into my mind. Feeling a hand on my shoulder, I turned to find three holy men. They said, "Walk with us." We went to the crest of a small hill behind the church and sat to watch the sunset. In unison they said, "The sun has set like the first sun, morning will come like the first morning."

The holy men stood and led the way down to a river where they carefully undressed, making neat piles of their clothes in a darkness barely lit by fireflies and a sliver of moon. They jumped into the river and laughed and splashed. After a bit, they silently came out, dressed and walked off. I jumped up, tore off my clothes and leapt into the dark, moving water. Ellie was right behind me. She cried out when a frog tangled in her hair and I laughed as she grabbed me tightly. The delicious intimacy of skin on skin was interrupted as Ellie cupped her hands and splashed a wave of water into my face and swam off.

Finally, we decided to climb out and drink the wine and eat the cheese that the Old Woman told us to bring. The intimacy of our connection and the warm rushing water had, unknown to us, washed us well down river. We stumbled from the river, our feet slipping on muddy vines. Laughing at our dilemma, Ellie held my hand and I felt her warm breath in my nostrils. I started to realize the magnitude of our dilemma when a Jeep's headlights flashed into our eyes and brought us back to reality. The driver was a monk from the church who said, "You silly people. Do you know where you are? Jump in and I'll take you back."

As the cool air dried my face and hair, I could feel Ellie's warmth as she leaned her head on my shoulder, her soft hair tickled my face. I had never understood the human need for touch and intimacy. This night my skin and senses were alive like no other time I could remember.

Our driver stopped at the church and we got out. Ellie and I were led to separate rooms at the rectory.

That night I dreamt in color. I was drifting through clouds where people of all sorts pulled a thread from their chest and pushed it through my heart where it turned gold and shimmered. Soon my chest had hundreds of gold threads connecting me to every person I saw. Then, as if playing a movie backwards, I flew down a tunnel and landed on the bed, my head dizzy. I woke up and felt my chest for the strings. Seeing no light outside my window and still exhausted, I fell quickly back to sleep.

Later that same night, dreaming, I opened my eyes to a room filled with brown- and orange-robed monks, all lying on mats neatly arranged on the floor, inches apart. I was in the middle and could look in all directions and see nothing but monks. Still desperately tired I wondered what they would do when they found me, a non-monk among them in the morning. Suddenly, the flat stone ceiling of the sleeping chamber collapsed, and I, out of my body, looked down to see the room filled with red blood, except where I had slept—there I saw blue.

The dream was without emotional reponses or fear. The blue color that I was seemed as natural as breathing. I again fell off to sleep, my heart pried open by the secure night air.

Despair

I AWOKE DRENCHED in sweat, finding the sun beating on my body with its heat and my heart pounding. I recalled the last few days' events: the car ride, the church, the tears, the holy men, the swim, and Ellie's touch. I recalled the dreams of that night and they filled me with fear. I cried outloud, "I cannot bear to be human." I pulled my knees to my chest and huddled on the bed.

The sun was bright and I heard Ellie whispering outside my door, "Do you think he's awake? Gosh, it's almost noon, should we wake him?" I walked to the door and swung it open to find Ellie with Cell Phone Mama. They both jumped.

I looked at Cell Phone Mama, "Why are you here?" I asked.

She smiled as if illuminating the punch line of a joke, "I'm her mother."

Ellie's mother held the paintings and sketches of the Old Woman who brought me chocolate and a beating. She said, "Would you sign the front of these? A museum wishes to display them and says they must be signed."

I glanced at the painted sketches and said without thinking, "These are not mine, the person that painted them is dead."

Ellie grabbed my hands angrily and held them out. "Did these hands, did this finger," she grabbed my index finger, bending it back, "touch the pens, pencils and brushes that made these?"

I said nothing. Ellie bent my finger back until it became numb, but I remained silent.

Finally, she released my finger and cried to her mother, "I thought he was a kind man but he is just an ass. A self-absorbed fool who can't get out of his head!"

Ellie grabbed the pictures and the brushes and ink her mom had brought for me to sign with, and threw them in my face and left. I looked at the paintings again and wrote on each one in the finest pen I knew, "A self-absorbed ass stuck in his head."

French Colors

I TOOK THE PAINTINGS to the window and seeing Ellie and her mother, started tossing them out. They swayed back and forth falling to Ellie who caught them. Upon reading my recently scribed and still wet "self-absorbed ass" signature, Ellie ran back up to my room with a red face and obscene gestures. She raged in a voice so loud I could hear the neighborhood dogs and chickens bark and cackle, upset with her screams.

Ellie's anger seemed to come from her belly and take control. Spit came out of her mouth as she barked words at me, "Connard! Fils de pute! La putain de ta mère!" For good or bad, I had learned French on the streets of Paris as a youth. I understood how vile her words painted me and my character.

Ellie's voice grew hoarse as her lecture continued. She talked about her Grandma, God, my stupidity, my intellectual emptiness, how I was just a brain with no heart and not human. I grabbed a painting from Ellie and wrote on it and handed it back. She paused for a minute and read my note outloud, "I want to be Ellie's friend. Old Woman, I want to be her real friend."

"Your words," she hoarsely whispered, "are intellectual words like a monkey trained to do and say the right things. And besides, you fool, Grandma's dead!"

I grabbed another painting and wrote:

Ellie, please look in my eyes.
Do you see love?
Do you see God?
Do you see a human who is learning to

She snatched the painting before I could finish my scribbles, read it and grabbed my face, her fingernails piercing deep in the skin of my cheeks. I felt the old woman's presence in the room as I looked into Ellie's eyes, "Ellie I'm sorry. I realize you loved your Grandmother very much."

Reality

FROM THE DOORWAY, Cell Phone Mama softly said, "Emmanuel, it is hard to be human, but it's reality." She quietly came in the room, motioned for me to lay down and placed her hand over my heart. Cell Phone Mama told Ellie to come over to the bed and to place her hands over my cold fingers that were crossed on my stomach. As if in a ritual, Cell Phone Mama placed her other hand over my eyes and began murmuring a prayer. I became lightheaded.

Ellie's mother, in a firm yet gentle voice, said "Concentrate on your breathing…hear my words…feel the light go through the hands on your head, heart and stomach, breathe with your stomach! Breathe!"

I breathed, my head felt light, warmth filled my chest, as Ellie's mother kissed my lips, she pulled Ellie close and said, "Ellie, last night, the Emmanuel that painted those pictures died. This is no more him than I am you. Let it go."

As if in an electrical flash, I felt my being smash-
ed into a blue puddle. I felt warmth and comfort
and no fear.

Cell Phone Mama continued, "Emmanuel, this
is going to sound like a lecture but it is not. I am
speaking what my hands are uncovering in your
heart and mind."

I smiled at her, to let her know I understood her
words.

She continued, "Our most intimate Self, our most
vulnerable Self, is our spiritual Self. Yet, it is our
strongest Self. We think we can be protected from
suffering by cloaking our spirit in activities and
intellectual symbols. Fear causes this and the fear
is simply a cover-up for, as Ellie so eloquently put
it, pompous, egotistical idiots who are ultimately
afraid to be human.

You say God is real, but as sentient humans to us
it's really God's expression that is real."

She gently pushed Ellie away, leaned over me and
grabbed my hair with both her hands. "Emmanuel,
love is real and we must live and love like we will
never be hurt, without fear." She then pulled hard
and said a bit louder, "What did I just say?"

"God is love, we must express love without fear. We must live and love like we will never be hurt!"

Cell Phone Mama smiled big, relaxed her grip on my hair, then pulled it hard again and said, "When must we express love without fear?"

I answered, "Always."

She stood up and said, "Aren't you two supposed to be somewhere?" She left with the Old Woman paintings under her arms.

Promise

"MAMA'S RIGHT," Ellie smiled, "I promised my Grandma I'd take you to the end of the map." As we drove, I wrote my first poem titled "I Love Like I've Never Been Hurt." I later changed the title to "Innocence."

The map led us to a large orphanage. As Ellie and I walked up the stairs, we were greeted by a smiling, and nearly perfectly round nun who smelled like Ivory soap and babbled, "I knew you would come, I knew you would come."

I said, "Madam, it is impossible for you to know we would be here." She pulled out a letter and handed it to me. It said:

Dear Sister Agnes, my granddaughter, Ellie, will bring a quiet man to your orphanage on July 11th, please take him inside your walls, and give him this broom and say it is the beating broom and laugh (he

will understand). Make sure he has 64 colored pencils
and white paper. Take him into the garden and invite
him to sit. Ask Ellie to leave, she will resist but you
must be firm, tell her Dr. Emmanuel will take a taxi
back. Once Ellie has gone, please let the children into
the garden. Ask Dr. Emmanuel to give each child a
pencil, 64 should do it exactly.

In the garden, the children gathered around
me, touching my face to see if I was real. I
smiled and felt warmth in my chest. One of
the smallest children climbed into my lap
and said, "Are you really a saint?"

I laughed, "No, I am just plain
Emmanuel."

For the next hour, the children asked me
question after question, "Why is grass green?" "Are
you an artist?" "Have you ever had diarrhea?"

Then a small boy asked, "Do you have a father
and mother?"

The courtyard grew quiet as I searched for words.
I held his hand up to my heart and put my hand
over it, "My father and mother are in here."

A tall girl with freckles and braids said, "We are

all orphans. Sister Agnes says that's what makes us special."

Tears came to my eyes and a child asked me why I was crying.

I replied, "Because I'm a special orphan too. I think I could use 64 hugs." The children all crowded close to me. Some wiped my tears on their sleeves before the hug, some gave soft kisses on my cheek, some gave quick pats-on-my-back hugs, others, bear hugs. Then Sister Agnes came up and laughed, "Let's make it an even 65!"

She whispered in my ear, "Let's talk privately," and asked the children to draw while we excused ourselves.

In an office filled with files and pictures of children, Sister Agnes shared a beautiful vision of how my life would unfold. She had seen it in a dream. I carefully listened, feeling afraid, happy and a bit embarrassed. When she was done, although I knew she expected a reply, I said nothing, hugged her, and quickly left without saying goodbye to the children.

Unbearable Love

I WALKED 5 KM to the nearest town and hired a
driver to take me back to my studio home. When I
arrived, Ellie was sitting on my steps. She blushed
and handed me a letter. It was in her handwriting
and said:

Love
Just Love
Let Love guide you
Love with joy
Love when happy
Love when sad
Trust and let Love teach you how to express Love

The letter was puckered from dried tears. It went on:

Emmanuel, I am not an artist or an eloquent writer
with PhDs. But I can tell you, don't be afraid. I look

deep into myself and deep into you and I see such joy,
such kindness, such love, yet your fear, your ego, clings
to stupid PhD concepts of love and God and life. God's
will is that we live fully, be happy and wish safety, love,
and happiness for and expressed to all. I hope you'll
smile at life and let the connection happen. God is one
with you! God's will...

Blessings,

Ellie

Primary Colors

ELLIE REACHED FOR my hand and slowly led me into my apartment. I did not speak. She laid me down on the bed and asked if I was comfortable. As she pulled the sandals from my feet, tears welled up in my eyes. Ellie climbed on my stomach and wiped my tears away with her palms. She stared down into my eyes and said nothing. I could not bear the intimate connection and truth that seemed to flow through our eyes, between us. I closed my eyes tight. Ellie laid her head against my chest, her petite body fit comfortably against my slender build and soon we fell into a deep sleep.

I dreamt of children dressed in 64 colors with opaque white tears streaming from their smiling faces. Suddenly everything went white—the children, my clothing, and all my surroundings had no dimension, time, space, color, or mass. In my hand

I held three brushes dripping in red, blue, and yellow; before me lay thick white paper. I could create any life I wanted. Filled with art, with children, with Ellie, with God.

The clock said 6 o' clock as the warm morning sun woke me as I lay next to Ellie. I quietly breathed in the clean air and then sat up and grabbed a Lindt chocolate bar. The pink sunrise illuminated Ellie's face. I counted her breaths, six per minute, she was deeply asleep. I wanted to tell her about the dream. I filled my mouth with the candy bar and softly blew chocolate breaths a few centimeters from her face. She did not awaken. I pulled myself close to her and delicately traced her lips with my tongue covered in chocolate's sweetness. She lay still, breathing six breaths a minute.

Would this girl never wake up? I thought.

I carefully whispered in her ear, "Ellie, I just dreamed I was born a happy man," and kissed the tip of her earlobe.

Suddenly, she reached her arm around me and murmured, "Emmanuel, we choose happiness." And promptly fell back asleep with a smile curving on her brown-painted lips.

I sighed and counted her breaths again. I wondered if I should leave her alone and wrapped myself around her warm body.

"Quit counting and kiss me Mr. Happiness..." she whispered.

"I love you, Ellie," I said.

"I know," she replied.

La Fin

What Others Said about Emmanuel's Prayer

Certainly, if I were alive, and Paul Sutherland dead,
or even alive, Emmanuel's Prayer *would be about the*
drunken savage Voltaire, and, along with its title and
words all changed, as rose petals brown in the sun.
—William Shakespeare

Just because Paul Sutherland wrote it doesn't mean I'll
read it! Which I won't! Not because I don't read—but
because I take offense at the title. Emmanuel's Prayer.
What's that? —George Bernard Shaw

Last night I read Emmanuel's Prayer *to its last page,*
and, then I read it again before I blew out the candle.
I read it again this morning and gave it to my sister.
I must say it is missing a sentence or two, which, even
after my sister and I looked, we cannot find.
—Bertrand Russell

Paul, context: This should have been placed in Iowa or upstate New York with names like Bob, and well, Ellie I guess is okay, but not Emmanuel. I hope someone buys it. —Carl Sandburg

I hope your editors did not remove any words. Certainly, if I had edited Emmanuel's Prayer *it would be a three-volume tome. But on second thought, I get it. You let me, the reader, use my imagination! My, how refreshing. —Erica Jong*

I hope Paul Sutherland does not hope to sell Emmanuel's Prayer *in the Americas. Europeans will find his prose ripe to illuminate their imaginations, and love the work. Americans, while they have vision (they lack imagination), will need more explanation to get its essential truths. —Alexis de Tocqueville*

Was Emmanuel a vegetarian? Was he named after Swedenborg and the Tiaze monks? If so, tell us! I wanted to know Emmanuel. —Henry David Thoreau

Emmanuel's Prayer *is sentimental rubbish.*
—Leo Tolstoy

I think your book is 50% better than one half good. My sister-in-law's drunk husband read me every word. Then, because he can't think and read aloud at the same time, he read it again silently. All he did was read then look at me teary-eyed and say "I'm not crying... dry air." —Mark Twain

I cried as I read your book. Were Emmanuel and Ellie lonely? Essentially, I think your book should be called literature. —Nathaniel West

Emmanuel's Prayer *will sell well, but only because it is one word away from poetry. Prose sells, poetry, like poems, sits on the shelf.* —Emily Dickinson

My word! Paul Sutherland, where are the words? Do you not know writers get paid by the number of words? Literature is full of words, did you lose some? Go find some and look up "descriptive" in the dictionary. Then, rewrite Emmanuel's Prayer *and I shall write the best review of any ever written.* —Gertrude Stein

I had wondered where my angel of allegory had gone; now I know! The angel resides at Paul Sutherland's house or offices. My allegory angel abandoned me the day I died, the fickle fellow. Next work, Mr. Sutherland should learn to use his words with less volume. But, often in youth, we oversay and understate. —Edmund Spenser

Blood, blood, blood! Mr. Sutherland, once you spill blood in your books, you need to let your reader taste blood, feel blood, wash in the blood. Go rewrite

Emmanuels' *bloody parts and I'll recommend your book and buy one for my neighbor. By the way, consider calling* Emmanuel's Prayer: Bloody Emmanuel. *You'll sell more copies and people, especially Americans, love blood.*—Edgar Allan Poe

In Emmanuel's Prayer II, *please develop Ellie's character more. She is the meat and love of* Emmanuel's Prayer. *If T.S. were alive, he would have enjoyed your book. I would give it as a gift, of course.*
—Vivienne Eliot

I think Christians will love the book, Emmanuel's Prayer, *and hate Paul Sutherland's rude irreverence. After all, I am not here to write this review and if I were, Paul is merely inferring what I would say. Which I am, of course.* —C. S. Lewis

Trilogy, Mr. Sutherland, trilogy. What's next? What happens to Ellie and Emmanuel? Does he buy her a precious gold ring? If I were alive, I'd send you one of mine. My animal spirits were aroused when I read this book. —J.R.R. Tolkien

One Love

Long ago
Maybe lifetimes...
        I learned to listen
        I learned to see
        I learned to smell
        I learned to taste
        I learned to feel

Then I learned to think
        Big thinking thoughts I learned

I listened to those thoughts
Thoughts told me what to listen to
Thoughts told me what to see
Thoughts told me what to smell
Thoughts told me what to taste
Thoughts told me what to feel

        My ears grew small
        My eyes turned gray and closed
        My nose turned to stone
        My tongue to velvet
        My skin was covered by cotton

My thoughts became me

Then a woman of love and power
Saw her wisdom reflected in my covered heart
She took fire and water
Air and earth
And covered me with their essence
Bound together with her blood and spit

She wiped this moisture on
My ears
Nose
Tongue
Eyes
And skin

My thoughts said run
But I could not run
I was blind
I only know the power was
From a woman
By her smell of life that filled
My lungs, my mouth, my heart
Even today I feel this smell
But I forgot the smell
And fell into
Fire, ice, and earth
Through air and wind
And was wrapped for
Years days months so tight

That thoughts did not think
Thinking had no thoughts
Beginnings had no ends
Ends had no beginnings
Nothing was real
And real was nothing
I floated through this life
       And wondered
Will I smell her smell again
Will I hear her soft breaths on my face
Will her lips touch mine once more
Will tongues embrace and skin become one
Will I close my eyes and see her
Will I remember? I feared I would forget...

Long ago
I learned to listen
I heard love

Long ago
I learned to see
I saw love

Long ago
I learned to smell
I smelled love

Long ago
I learned to taste
I tasted love

Long ago
I learned to feel
I felt love

My thoughts
        Allowed me to forget
My ears, my eyes, my nose, tongue, skin and
Heart did not forget

        A warm sun reflected
        On 2 hearts
        2 tongues
        2 bodies
Warming them to release
Fire, earth, air and water

To Let hearts
        Tell them how to see
To let hearts
        Allow them to listen
To let hearts unite
        In one taste
        One smell
        One skin
        One

One love

Long, long long ago about one second or more ago
        Love was there

I see now that
>Love was always there to see

I hear now
>Love's song has always been

My nose
>Taught me that love's aroma is here always

My tongue
>Tastes love deep and sweet

My skin
>Feels no separation from love

>How can I be

So bold about love
>How can I with

Confidence and optimism
>Say such truths about love...

Simple really...
>I met my true love.

Sometimes when I pray
I use words...
—St. Francis de Assisi